Midnight
CALLER

Short stories by
MARCIA ELIZABETH ROSE

Midnight
CALLER

Short stories by
MARCIA ELIZABETH ROSE

MEREO
Cirencester

Mereo Books

1A The Wool Market Dyer Street Cirencester Gloucestershire GL7 2PR
An imprint of Memoirs Publishing www.mereobooks.com

Midnight Caller: 978-1-86151-882-8

First published in Great Britain in 2016
by Mereo Books, an imprint of Memoirs Publishing

The address for Memoirs Publishing Group Limited can be found at
www.memoirspublishing.com

The Memoirs Publishing Group Ltd Reg. No. 7834348

The Memoirs Publishing Group supports both The Forest Stewardship Council® (FSC®) and the PEFC® leading international forest-certification organisations. Our books carrying both the FSC label and the PEFC® and are printed on FSC®-certified paper. FSC® is the only forest-certification scheme supported by the leading environmental organisations including Greenpeace. Our paper procurement policy can be found at www.memoirspublishing.com/environment

Typeset in 12/18pt Plantin
by Wiltshire Associates Publisher Services Ltd. Printed and bound in Great Britain by Printondemand-Worldwide, Peterborough PE2 6XD

CONTENTS

FREEDOM

It was as if time stood still. Was it still only four o'clock on a Sunday afternoon? Lisa felt that she had been waiting all her life for this moment and now that the time had come, it seemed to be passing so very slowly. Could this really be happening? Was she finally going to be free? And what world was she returning to?

Lisa had been very scared and frightened when she had entered prison 20 years before as a young woman of 26. She had dreamed every day of being released. She could hardly believe that this was not just another dream, and that she really was about to cross the border to Switzerland and into safety.

It seemed to take forever to walk across the bridge that would lead her to freedom. As she walked, she felt terribly afraid that this could be a trick and she might find herself bundled back into another prison. Her mind was in a muddle. She could not take in the big bridge that loomed before her. Everything around seemed surreal and huge.

Nothing could have prepared her for what lay ahead. As the other prisoner passed her, he pulled out a knife and stabbed her in her shoulder. At first she didn't even feel the blade going through, until she heard a loud crack and realised that it had dug into the bone. One minute she was standing next to the man and the next she was on the ground in a pool of blood. Lying beside her was the man who had stabbed her. She did not even realise that he had fallen too, and that the crack had been the sound of a shot. She was in such a weak state that the force of the blade going into her shoulder had simply knocked her to the ground.

She lay stunned, drifting into unconsciousness, with blood pouring from her wound. Briefly she wondered if it was worth fighting to live. Maybe she should just let the blackness enfold her, forever...

Helpless, she slipped into a coma.

Lisa had always wanted to join the Army, and she

had signed up as soon as she was 18. She was an excellent soldier and had worked her way up in the ranks until eventually she was trusted enough to be asked to go undercover for her country. She proved to be a very good spy, being skilled at languages and at blending into her surroundings so that she was not noticed. She had passed back all the knowledge she had gained from her contacts, until one day she had got caught. She had hoped desperately that after a few days or weeks her government would rescue her, but it never happened. She was constantly moved to different caves or holes, and some of the places where she was imprisoned she endured great torture.

Eventually, without any trial, she ended up in a women's prison. It was appallingly squalid and she had very little food or water. Dehydration and stomach pains were a constant reminder of her situation. Every day she dreamt of her freedom, always believing that one day she would be rescued, but as the years passed she had come to the conclusion that she was never going to get back home. Her efforts were spent in trying to keep herself alive and as well as possible, which was very difficult.

She knew that they could kill her at any time. The torture was awful, but they always stopped before it went too far, which made her wonder – why am I still alive? Am I a bargaining chip? This gave her hope, even though they continued to parade her around like a trophy with her hands tied together with rope and her head shaved, and made her walk for miles around the camp, whipping her and spitting at her. Lisa just kept telling herself, *they need you alive, don't be concerned with the pain, it means you are still alive. You will heal.* She constantly prayed for help and the strength to endure her ordeal. Her faith became her life support.

Eventually she was sent to another prison and the torture stopped altogether, which was an answer to her prayers. It gave her time to heal.

And then the day they came when they told her she was going home. They pushed her into a shower cubicle, shaved off what little hair she had left, washed her down with soap and gave a pair of old trousers and a vest top. After being carried in a Jeep, blindfolded, for hours, she was released at the side of the bridge and the blindfold was taken off.

After a while she woke up, feeling totally confused. She couldn't remember where she was. She saw a man in a white coat at her bedside and thought he was a doctor, but she could not be sure. He had a kind face and was smiling, but this made her more fearful as she was not used to anyone being kind to her.

The doctor explained to her what had happened. His first words to her were, "Lisa, you are in Switzerland. You are not in prison any more. You are in hospital and you are safe". He went on to explain that she had a severe shoulder injury and was recovering from surgery. He also told her that she had been in a coma for two weeks and during that time they had helped to keep her alive and build her up by feeding her by tube with food and vitamins. They had operated on her shoulder and repaired it. Now it was time for the tube to be taken out and for her to eat and get stronger; eventually she would be able to start some gentle physiotherapy exercises for her arm. He said that with physio her arm would be back to normal in a few weeks' time. In the meantime she was to eat, and to try just to sit up for the first few days, and then when she was a little stronger she could try walking carefully around the bed. Eventually she would be able to walk outside in the hospital grounds and get herself strong and well again. Apart from the injuries, she was suffering from exhaustion and malnutrition.

In due course the physiotherapy helped Lisa's arm to get back to normal. She greatly enjoyed her walks outside in the mountain air and began to feel restored and fit for the first time in 20 years. She also put on some weight, which made a big difference, as she had previously looked like a skeleton.

When she was well enough, she was summoned for a debriefing. They told her that the US government had been trying for years to rescue her, but every time they had found out where she was the enemy had moved her to another prison. Then they had received a request for a criminal they were keeping in prison to be released in exchange for Lisa, and a deal was done. They had not realised that during the exchange the prisoner had had a knife, but they had been expecting something to happen, so they had a helicopter team on standby with a command to shoot and kill the man if Lisa was harmed in any way. So when they saw Lisa fall to the ground, they had immediately opened fire on the other prisoner and killed him. Soldiers had run onto the bridge and covered both bodies with red blankets. They had then pronounced them both dead at the scene, so her captors watching on the other side of the bridge would believe that both prisoners had been killed.

When her captors saw this they opened fire on the helicopter, but it was already out of range, so they retreated back to their side of the border and drove off in their Jeep. Lisa had then been taken immediately into the waiting ambulance and rushed into surgery. Now that she had been pronounced dead there was no question of taking her back to the USA, so a grave was dug for her in the military cemetery in Washington with her full name and rank. On her headstone were the words: "Here lies a valiant soldier who died serving her country. RIP."

The funeral ceremony had taken place in Washington with full military honours, and then Lisa was given a new name and allowed to choose any country of her choice to live in. Sadly her parents had died a few years earlier, and she was an only child, so she decided to stay in Switzerland. The US government paid for all her expenses and gave her a beautiful log cabin at the foot of the mountains. They also paid her backdated Army pension and gave her full compensation.

Although she had retired from the Army, the soldiers who had served with her visited her regularly, and she liked cooking for them. She felt they were her brothers and sisters, and were now her true family. They enjoyed her company and her cooking too. Because food had been so scarce for Lisa over so many years, she now loved to cook, and especially for her Army family.

She spent the rest of her life living a mainly

solitary life in Switzerland, which continued to suit her for the next ten years. She loved climbing the local hills and mountains. She also wrote a book about her life in prison, which was published after her death. It was a remarkable story of one woman's endurance against all the odds. She survived and overcame more than any person normally could, because of her faith in God and the belief in herself, her training and her countrymen. At Lisa's request, her ashes were scattered by helicopter over her favourite mountain by a small gathering of her friends.

Her book, which was titled 'Hope', became a best-seller worldwide and the money from sales went to help veteran soldiers who had sustained injuries or mental trauma during their time of service in the Army, and to pay for the help needed for them to adjust to civilian life again.

THE ROBBERY

Why on earth could Marie not sleep? It was two o'clock in the morning, and all she could do was toss and turn, trying desperately to drift off. However she tried, she just could not manage it.

After a while she got up and made herself some chamomile tea, then put some lavender oil on her pillow and started counting sheep, for the hundredth time that night. But nothing did any good. It was not as if anything was worrying her; she was just not tired. Yet she knew that if she did not drift off soon, when morning came she would be tired and exhausted, just as she was every morning.

It wasn't as if she had done anything wrong – had she? Yes, she had agreed to get some money from the bank where she worked to help her sister Janet, but surely anyone would help their own sister out if she needed help. And Janet needed her help badly, because she needed to have an expensive operation. That was why she had come to Marie.

Marie was Assistant Manager of her local branch, and she dealt with money every day. The bank would not miss a few thousand pounds, surely. Five thousand pounds, to be exact. After all, they trusted her to close all the takings at the end of the day. She had all the codes for the vaults, and it wasn't as if she was stealing from people who needed the money. She would only take money from very wealthy clients who had plenty in their accounts, so they were unlikely to miss a few thousand pounds. At least, that's what she kept telling herself. After all, Janet needed her, and she couldn't turn her back on her sister when she so desperately needed this operation.

They had found a brilliant surgeon in Harley Street who could undertake the surgery, but he said it did mean that they would have to go to his private clinic in Austria. This was the only hope they had, and the operation would be very expensive. Yet the surgery could change her sister's life, and it was not available in Scotland or England. Janet and Marie had no choice but to agree.

Getting the money was the problem. Janet was on sick leave from the local infant school where she worked, so it was down to Marie to come up with a bank loan. An unofficial one. After all it was purely for medical reasons, and she was going to try and pay it back as soon as she could. As long as the bank didn't miss the money, all would be well.

Marie started taking the money a bit at a time, a couple of hundred pounds a week from each person she had decided could afford it, until after five weeks she finally had the £5,000 she needed to pay for the operation. No one had detected the missing money, and she had not been caught, so why was she so worried now? Maybe it was because the rucksack containing the last instalment was still in her bedroom. She felt guilty every time she looked at it, but after tomorrow it would be gone.

It was Friday, and she did not have to work. All she had to do was get to sleep, then in the morning she would go to the post office, where she had arranged for the money to be paid by transfer. She had been transferring the money for the treatment every Friday and today was the last instalment. Then all she had to do was catch the flight to Austria on

Saturday afternoon. All being well, they would stay in Austria for a week while her sister had her treatment, and then Marie would return to work the following week.

Marie and Janet lived together. They had always been close, especially since their parents had died when they were teenagers. Marie was the elder by three years, so she felt responsible for Janet. They didn't have any other family, so this was the only course open to them. As long as the bank didn't miss the money before her treatment, they would be all right. If however they were found out and stopped at the airport, Marie knew that she would have to go to prison and her sister would not get her vital operation. The thought of this was the main reason why Marie could sleep. The other reason was that she did not yet have any idea how she could give the money back, and that was a major concern.

Her sister knew nothing about how Marie had got the money. As far as she was concerned, her sister had taken out a bank loan. Well, that was true, in a sense; it just wasn't the usual kind.

Now all she had to do was sleep until the morning. If only she could stop her brain from turning everything over and somehow manage to drop off, she would be OK. She reached out and set her alarm for 9 am, and eventually she fell into a deep sleep.

The next thing she knew, the alarm was ringing and it was time to get up. She quickly had a shower and changed into her jeans and T-shirt, had a cup of coffee and left the house to go to the post office.

Normally she was able to go straight to the counter and arrange the money transfer, but today there was a queue and she had to wait in line with four people in front of her. She started to get very agitated. It was imperative that the last of the money should go through today without any complications.

Eventually, after a long wait, Marie reached the counter and the money transfer went through without any problem, which was a great relief to her. Greatly relieved, she left the post office and walked back home, feeling so much better than she had the previous night. Now all she had to do was return to her flat, where her sister would be waiting for her to finish her packing, and book the taxi to the airport for tomorrow. So far, so good.

They arrived at the airport in plenty of time for their flight, although Marie was very relieved when they managed to get through customs without being stopped. She only really relaxed once the plane had taken off and they were on their way. She now knew her sister really would be having the treatment she needed to make her well again.

After a week of intensive treatment, Janet was discharged from the hospital and was allowed to travel back home. She was very frail after her treatment and Marie could not wait to get her back home to Scotland again. When they arrived at the airport, Marie went into the duty-free shop to get some gifts of Austrian and Swiss chocolates to take into work on Monday. She had already told Mr Prendergast, her boss, that she was going to Austria as her sister had been unwell and she had decided that the fresh mountain air would help her feel better after her recent virus. She felt it would be best to explain the reason why she had chosen Austria before leaving, so he would not ask too many questions about her holiday when she returned. She had taken care to read up all about the area they were going to so that she would be able to answer any questions she might be asked. She had explained that they had booked a small cabin at the foot of a mountain near the lake for a peaceful and restful break. Marie thought that would stop him asking more about her holiday. In truth she had hardly seen anything of Austria, because most of her time had been spent at her sister's bedside at the hospital.

After their flight they arrived back home safely and she was relieved that her sister had managed so well during the long journey. They unpacked their suitcases, showered and got into their pyjamas. They were both exhausted and they went straight off to bed, even though it was only 6 pm.

Marie had just managed to get to sleep when her mobile phone rang. It was Mr Prendergast, informing her that the bank had been robbed. She was awake immediately. He explained that he had been on his way in, but there had been an accident on the motorway and he was going to be delayed by at least half an hour, so could she please go in as soon as possible, as she lived around the corner from the bank and she had a copy of the master key. He said the police had been called.

Marie quickly wrote a note to her sister, as she did not want Janet to wake up and find that she was not home. Then she dressed and walked to the bank, feeling sick and scared that she might finally be found out. But when she entered the building, she found dust and furniture turned upside down. The safe door had been blown open by a big explosion and there was concrete dust everywhere. It looked as if the robbers had drilled through from the pizza café next door.

Marie peered around, very frightened in case the robbers were still on the premises, but to her relief it was clear that they had long since left the bank. She carefully went to the safe and found the door open. She saw that all the drawers of the safe deposit boxes had been forced open, and some of the money was scattered on the floor, obviously dropped by the robbers in their haste to leave. She looked carefully through the safe deposit boxes and saw that all the boxes she had previously stolen from had been broken into. She left the area and returned to her office.

Just as she reached her office door a police car squealed up with siren blaring, and the bank was suddenly full of police. She told them that she had looked in to see the damage but had not touched anything. The officer in charge asked her to draw up a list of every account with the total that had previously been in the safe deposit boxes, so that they could see how much had been taken. It was then that Mr Prendergast arrived.

It had already occurred to Marie that if she pretended that the safety deposit boxes had still contained the correct amount before the robbery – the amount that had been there before Marie had taken the money for her sister – no one would ever know what she had done. The robbers would get the blame for taking all the money. After all, as far as her clients or her boss were aware the amount of money that was registered was the amount that was still in the safe deposit boxes at the time of the robbery.

The bank was sealed for a week while the investigation continued. Over the next few days Marie worked very hard to put together a full report on just how much money and jewellery was in each of the safe deposit boxes. Eventually she had a full list of all the account details, with the names and addresses of all the clients that had safe deposit boxes with the bank, along with a full itinerary of their contents, which she gave to the police.

After a few weeks of investigating, the police arrested Mr Prendergast. They had discovered that the security cameras had not been operating over the weekend. In truth, her boss had nothing to do with the robbery. He had merely forgotten to put the cameras on when he left on Friday evening. Marie gave evidence that she was the one that always cashed up after work and was responsible for putting the cameras on, but on this occasion she had been away on holiday. The police accepted her account, and they soon cleared her of any involvement.

The robbery had been discovered because the

pizza shop manager was unable to open his shop in the day due to staff sickness, so he decided to open just for the evening. When he had reached the shop he had gone into the basement and seen the hole that had been knocked through into the bank. He had then phoned the police.

There was no evidence that Mr Prendergast had deliberately left the alarm system off to help the robbers, so he was not charged with any offence, but he was in serious trouble with the bank for failing in his duty. They ruled that it was the responsibility of the manager at all times to make the premises secure. Although they accepted that it had been an oversight on his part, he was still responsible for security as the manager of the branch, so he was asked to resign. The police then closed the file, because the robbers could not be identified as the cameras had been turned off.

Marie was relieved that because there was no record of any money missing before the robbery, she did not have to worry about paying back the cash she had 'borrowed'. Head office ordered that better security was needed before the bank could open again. This meant that high-level security had to be installed into the bank and CCTV cameras were on automatically 24 hours a day.

Marie was invited to apply for the post of manager

to replace Mr Prendergast. She was now on much higher pay than she had ever had been before. Every month she saved a large part of her salary, and eventually after many months she had five thousand pounds in her savings account. She wanted to keep this in case her sister ever needed further treatment in the future. She vowed she would never steal again. She had been very fortunate that the robbers had chosen her bank, and also that her crime could not be traced back to her.

Fortunately Janet recovered well and did not need any more treatment, and Marie never stole again. The five thousand pounds she had managed to save was never spent, but she kept it in her savings account as a reminder to her that their lives would have been very different if she had been caught.

Mr Prendergast moved to the south of France with his wife, where he bought a small vineyard and enjoyed tending it. Before he left, he said to Marie that he could have easily been sent to prison, and he could not believe that he had forgotten to turn on the security cameras. He said he had relied too much on her to do it over the years, and because she had not been there he had simply forgotten. Fortunately he had some savings which enabled him to buy a small villa in his favourite part off France. He was therefore now pleased that the robbery had taken place, because it meant he was able to spend quality time with his wife and running their small winery.

Janet returned to working part-time at the local school, but she was looking forward to going back to working full time in the next few months. Marie was now able to sleep much better at night knowing her sister was well and she had promotion in the job she loved to do. It appeared to her that the robbery had indeed changed all of their lives for the better, and they were all financially secure, including, unfortunately, the robbers.

Another good thing was that Marie never struggled to get to sleep again.

MIDNIGHT CALLER

———❦———

If the phone rang again Susan was sure she would just throw it out of the window. She had only just moved into her sixth floor home in an apartment block in New York, and it had a land line telephone. Initially, she had been pleased to have it, because she had a poor signal on her mobile phone in the flat. It was the calls she was getting that were the problem.

It all started on the night she had moved in. When she answered the phone, all she heard was heavy breathing. At first it didn't bother her and she just put the phone down, but the calls went on, and lately she had been getting them every evening, always at midnight.

The next day was her day off work, so she decided to buy an answering machine so that she did not have to answer the phone every time it rang. The phone would never stop ringing until she answered. She set the machine to come on after one ring, and every morning when she woke up she saw the red light flashing on the telephone. Every time she played the message it was the same heavy breathing. It had been happening now for eight weeks. Susan decided that she would go to the police station after work and ask for any advice they could give her.

Susan was a single woman aged 35. She loved children and enjoyed working as a teacher, but after she had been at the school for a year she had had a very bad bicycle accident. A lorry pulled out in front of her and she was hit side on. She was in hospital for over two months recovering. She had broken ribs, a broken pelvis and leg and she had to have her spleen removed. Her injuries were very serious, and she was also told that due to the damage in her pelvis she would never be able to have or carry children. This was a devastating blow, as she had always imagined that one day she would have a family of her own.

After she had recovered from her injuries she started court proceedings against the driver and his company, which resulted in months of court hearings.

Finally the driver admitted liability and was banned from driving, and Susan was awarded a substantial amount of compensation. She went back home to her parents' home in Dorset to complete her recovery.

It was during this period of recuperation that she decided that she did not want to return to teaching because being with children every day would be a constant reminder that she could not have any herself, so she decided to start thinking of a career change. She had always been creative and had loved dressmaking and sewing, so while she was recovering she got back to using her old sewing machine and started designing outfits which she made for herself.

Then one day she saw that there was going to be a one-year dressmaking fashion course starting at the local college. After talking to her parents, she decided to enrol. She completed the course successfully and then decided to do a degree in fashion for a further two years at university. After gaining her honours degree, she saw an advertisement for a job as a fashion designer in New York. She applied and got the job, which came with an apartment. She was very nervous about working in New York as she didn't know anybody there, but fortunately the team welcomed her and made her time there very happy. It was very hard work, but she enjoyed the challenge.

After work the next day she decided to call into the police station regarding the phone calls. The young policeman on the desk was not very helpful and said it was probably just some kids messing around, but if she was still worried she should come back with the tapes from the answering machine and they would try and investigate it further.

After a couple of weeks Susan returned to the police station with the tapes and spoke to an older policeman who was much more helpful. However, after listening to the tapes the policeman said that he was sure that the heavy breathing was not that of a man but a child.

This really surprised Susan, and she asked what she should do, as when she spoke the person always hung up. The policeman said they would send someone around to see her the following day and try to work out what was happening.

The next day the policeman arrived with a file containing the papers for a case he had worked on two years before. It concerned the previous tenant of Susan's apartment, a woman with a daughter. The mother had been murdered by the janitor of the building in a rage, and her daughter had witnessed the crime. Apparently the mother and daughter had been playing hide and seek when the doorbell rang.

The mother had told the child to stay hidden while she answered the door. The child hid under the bed and through the opened door she saw her mother open the door and watched as a man stabbed her in the stomach. Her daughter bravely came out from under the bed when the man had left, and rang 911. She was crying and told them her mummy was hurt. When the police had arrived they had been too late to save the mother, and she was pronounced dead at the scene.

The child was taken into child services and questioned. When she was asked if she had seen anything she replied, "I saw Oscar hurt my mummy". The police immediately asked the other tenants who Oscar might be, and they told them that that was the name of the janitor at the apartments.

After a very long court hearing, the janitor was found guilty of murder and was sentenced to 30 years in prison. Upon leaving the dock as he was being taken down to his cell he called out to the little girl "I will kill you if you ever talk again. Remember that!" This was too much for the little girl and she ran from the court room. When they eventually found her she was sitting on the floor huddled up in a corner of the ladies' toilets. The child would not speak, and according to the police officer she had not spoken since that day. The child had no other family, so she was sent to a children's home. No one wanted to adopt her because she was a mute.

The policeman said that the case had therefore been closed, but there was always a possibility that one of Oscar's old fellow prisoners could be out playing tricks. He said he would test the phone line, and the next time the phone rang they would try and trace the call,. He said Susan would have to answer the phone and try and keep the person on the end of the line.

A few days later the phone rang once again at midnight. This time Susan answered the phone and asked who was calling and if they needed help. The line then went dead. The police said that the caller had not stayed on the line long enough for them to trace the call, but they would try again the next time it happened.

All over the weekend Susan waited for the phone to ring, but it never did and she became increasingly worried. The phone did not ring the following week either, so Susan decided to try and find out more about the little girl who had previously lived in her apartment. After doing some research she found out that the children's home that the little girl was staying in was only a few blocks from her apartment. Her name was Abigail Stevens.

The following weekend she decided to visit the home in order to find out more about Abigail. The home was a large house in private grounds, in a gated community. She approached the door and was let in by another couple who were just leaving the building. There was a very odd atmosphere about the place that Susan did not like. In the past Susan had visited many schools and establishments as a teacher, and compared to them this children's home seemed cold and uninviting. She asked if she could see Abigail and was immediately told she could not, as she was in solitary confinement for being naughty. The lady went on to say that Abigail was a handful and so she had to be punished.

Susan asked how old Abigail was and was informed that she was six years old. She was outraged that a child should be put into solitary confinement at such a young age. She then asked what had happened that was so awful to warrant her being punished in this way. The lady said she had been found using the office phone – at midnight. She added that she was baffled as to why Abigail wanted to use the phone, as she never spoke.

It was then clear to Susan that she had found her

mystery caller. She asked to see the child, but they would not allow it until tomorrow, once she was out of solitary. Susan made an appointment to come back and see her the next day.

It was a very long night for Susan, as she could not get Abigail out of her mind. She decided to go shopping and buy her a present to take the next morning. She took a colouring book, some crayons, a book about Winnie the Pooh and some sweets. She arrived at the home and was told she could only see Abigail for ten minutes. "She is mute, do not waste your time with her," the woman on duty said.

When Susan saw Abigail she was appalled at how tiny and skinny the girl was. Her clothes hung off her and she looked very frail and vulnerable. The look of hopelessness in the little girl's eyes melted her heart, and she just wanted to cuddle her and take her home.

Gently, she started to talk to Abigail and gave her the presents. The child seemed very shy, but she gave Susan a little smile as she left, and before Susan realised what she was doing she found herself marching into the matron's office, intending to demand that she should be allowed to adopt Abigail. There was no one there, but as she was waiting for the matron to return, Susan started wondering if she was doing the right thing. After all it was hardly appropriate to take the child back to the place where she had seen her mother murdered. What was she thinking?

Just then the matron came back, and Susan explained her plan. The matron agreed immediately. She warned her that Abigail was a sullen child and hard to please, but they would be glad for her to be taken off their hands.

Now of course Susan had a problem. What was she going to do with a six-year-old mute in New York, especially as she was working full time? She decided to phone her mother in the UK and talk it over with her. Her mother was very shocked at what Susan was planning to do, but she talked it over with her husband and they both said they were willing to support Susan and Abigail, and that if she wanted to come back home with the child, then they would be happy to have them living with them.

Susan did not want to leave New York or give up her job, having been so happy there, but she also could not bear the thought of a child being put into solitary confinement. And how could she get on with her life, knowing this child was so unhappy? She knew that she must return to the UK with Abigail. She felt that the quietness of the countryside would help her to heal, and as Susan had been a special needs teacher she felt she could home-school the girl and spend time with her one on one, helping her to learn how to speak again. She felt that with the love of Susan and her family around her, Abigail would have a chance of adapting better than in an apartment in New York.

So she started on the paperwork. It took three months for her to legally adopt Abigail and apply for a passport for her. During that time she visited the little girl regularly and told her all about her home back in England, saying that she would be going with her soon. During the visits Abigail never spoke, but there was a light in her eyes that had not been there before, and Susan was hopeful and pleased that she had made the right decision in deciding to take her back home. Susan felt that she must at least try to give this child a better future than she had experienced over the last two years, however long it might take.

On arriving at Susan's parents' house, Abigail was very nervous. She clung on to Susan and would not leave her side. Her mother bought in a tray of cold lemonade and together they sat in the conservatory overlooking the garden with their cups of tea and a tray of sandwiches and crisps for them all to enjoy. At first Abigail didn't want to eat the sandwiches, but with coaxing from Susan she finally tried them. She was soon enjoying the sandwiches and lemonade.

Then Susan suggested they should take a walk in the garden. It was a beautiful sunny day, and Susan took Abigail over to a very old swing that she had played on when she was a child. She lifted Abigail onto the swing and pushed her, and for the first time she saw a smile break out on Abigail's little face. Soon, for the very first time, she was laughing. It gave Susan a great sense of happiness that at last Abigail was learning to trust her.

Six months passed, and soon it was nearly Christmas. Abigail helped Susan and her grandparents decorate the tree and she did some baking with Susan's mum. They made trays of mince pies to give out to the carol singers. Afterwards Susan and her family went to the Christmas Eve service. The next day was Christmas Day, and after a wonderful traditional family roast dinner they sat down to open their presents. Susan was so happy and was really enjoying looking after her adopted daughter. The only problem was Abigail's continued near-silence. She would utter odd words here and there, but that was all.

Susan had now read an account of Abigail's mother's court case, which had been sent on to her, so she knew that the killer had told Abigail that if she ever spoke, he would kill her. She had taken this literally. Now it was all too clear why Abigail had been refusing to speak. The poor child must have been terrified ever since.

She realised that she had to explain to Abigail that it was now all right for her to speak and that no harm would come to her. She gently explained to the little girl that she could speak whenever she wanted to. The man was in prison, and in any case he could never find her, so she was not in any danger.

After they had finished unwrapping the many presents, Abigail ran to Susan and to her grandparents and hugged them all. Then, with a huge smile, she said "Thank you!"

After a few days Abigail was stringing sentences together, and by the time her seventh birthday came, she was speaking normally and had become very well adjusted. Susan's family loved her completely. The next step was to start school, so she was enrolled at the local school where Susan had previously worked. Before she started school, Susan made sure that the lessons she was teaching her were the same lessons as the school was following, so that when she started she would be up to the same level as the children who already started the previous term, if not higher.

After Susan had explained the child's situation to the head teacher, the woman asked her if she would consider coming back to work part time. Susan was delighted, because although she was in a different class from Abigail, she knew it would be good for her to be nearby if she was needed.

Abigail settled into school life very well, and Susan often wondered what her life would have been like if she had not had the accident which had resulted in her travelling to New York.

A year later, one evening when Susan and Abigail were cuddled up reading a story together she asked Abigail about the late-night phone calls. Abigail said she had hated being in the children's home. Every night at midnight the nurse would check to see if she was asleep and then go and sleep in the next room, leaving the office door open. Abigail remembered the telephone number of her house because her mother had taught her a song reciting the digits one by one, so that she would always remember the number if she ever got lost. She said she had been told that there was a new lady living in her old house now, so she would not be returning, but that she would be staying in the home until a new family chose to adopt her. She said she wanted to make sure that the lady living in her old house was safe. It was her way of checking that nobody else had been killed. As soon as she heard the woman's voice on the telephone, Abigail was happy, because she knew the woman was still safe. This made it easier for Abigail to keep quiet, believing that if she didn't speak the woman would be safe.

After hearing this story, Susan was moved to tears to think that she had been so cross, having believed that she was receiving nuisance calls when all along it was just a little girl making sure she was safe. Little had Susan known that by moving to New York she would meet and adopt a little girl of her own. Both their lives were now complete.

CREST OF THE WAVE

—◦⌣◦—

As Amelia Driscoll stood on the quayside looking towards where the ferry would be coming to drop off her next group of passengers, a speed boat roared past her and deliberately turned so that the waves covered her. She was drenched.

"You silly idiots!" she shouted out after them, but they just waved cheerily back at her. "Stupid boys!" she shouted, although she could see that they were not boys; they were grown men who had never grown up and who had more money than sense. They thought it was funny to soak a girl's clothes just for fun. That was what Amelia thought as she stood on the quayside soaked to the skin in the beautiful sunshine of Marbella. Great, she thought. How on earth was she going to explain this to the people she was meeting from the ferry?

Amelia worked as a holiday representative for a tour company in Marbella. She had only been in the job a month and was eager to make a good impression on her clients, as she was new to this job. She had not told her father back home what she was doing, as she knew he would disapprove.

She desperately tried to wring out her dress and rummaged in her bag to find a comb and mirror. Fortunately she had a head scarf in her bag, so she quickly used it to wrap her hair up into a small bun, hoping it would not be obvious that her hair was a wet mess underneath. She then applied more red lipstick. She was hoping that the ferry would be delayed, so that at least her dress could dry in the sun. Appearances were very important to the company she worked for and all the tour guides had to wear bright red lipstick and red nail varnish. Even their toenails had to be painted red, as they peeped out of her white sandals. The dress of her uniform and her scarf were white covered with small red polka dots, and her large handbag was red. The colour scheme was designed so that she could be easily recognised as the company's tour guide, and to make sure her group could not miss her. All she could do now was hope that her guests were too preoccupied with disembarking from the ferry to notice her disarray. Hopefully by the time she had them all on the air-conditioned coach it would be dry enough for her to sit down and welcome her guests for the half-hour coach drive to the hotel.

Just then she received a text from the captain of the ferry to say that because of a late passenger they had been delayed, and would be arriving in approximately 20 minutes instead of five. Amelia quickly texted the driver of the coach, who was also waiting for the passengers to arrive. As she now had time for a little more grooming, she quickly ran to the ladies' toilets to use the hand hair-dryers to try to dry her dress and as far as possible her hair. Fortunately it was not too wet now, and she managed to blow dry her fringe and then scraped her hair up into a pony tail. She then proceeded to dry the scarf before putting it back into her handbag. She was relieved to see how much better she looked, and she still had time to make it to the ferry drop-off in plenty of time to meet her guests.

Eventually the passengers arrived, and she escorted them onto the waiting air-conditioned coach. After everyone was seated, she started to explain about the journey they were going to be taking to arrive at their hotel.

Finally, after all her guests had been booked into their rooms, she was off duty and could go back to her hotel room for a shower. She took out a new dress ready for the morning. It was then that she switched on her TV.

The news was on, and she watched in horror as she saw that a speedboat had crashed into a liner and there had been a terrible fire. The speedboat occupants had all been killed. The liner had a hole in the side and was slowly taking in water, so they had summoned every available ship in the area to lift passengers off it. The pictures showed the remains of the speedboat, and Amelia was shocked to see that the name on the bow was *Crest of the Wave*. That was the boat which had got her soaked earlier that day! She felt awful that she had shouted at the occupants at the time, but also saddened that they had laughed at her warning for them to slow down. They had obviously continued driving much too fast and had collided with the liner a few minutes later, when they were further out at sea. She could only imagine that they must have been drinking too much alcohol, as they had had bottles of champagne in their hands earlier.

Just then her mobile phone rang. When she answered the call she was told to go immediately to the reception at the hotel, as there was a gentleman to see her and he had said it was urgent. On arriving at reception, Amelia was surprised to see her father waiting for her. This came as a big surprise, as she had not seen him for a year, although they had kept in touch with occasional phone calls or emails.

He was very agitated and quietly motioned her to sit in the corner of the bar area. She asked him what he was doing in Marbella and how he had known where to find her. He explained that he was there on business and had noticed her arrive at the hotel earlier in the evening. He was shocked to see that she was wearing a travel company uniform and asked her what she was doing working at the hotel. Amelia explained that she had wanted to work to earn her money rather than relying on his wealth to provide for her, and said she was enjoying her new job.

Her father was not at all impressed. He reminded her that she held a master's degree in finance, and she had not studied at university to be work as a rep with a travel company. The only reason he agreed for his daughter to attend university was so that she could join his business and eventually run it when he retired. Amelia had explained that she wanted to take a year off to explore before she joined her father's company, and she wanted to do it on her own, without her father's money. She had applied for a job in the travel business because she could speak several languages. Her father had reluctantly agreed to let her go ahead with this plan.

Neither Amelia nor her father noticed the man who was sitting in the shadows in a corner of the room, apparently reading a newspaper. As soon as Amelia and her father left, he made a call on his mobile phone and said quietly, "I've found her".

It was pure chance that the man in the shadows had stumbled upon Amelia. He had been looking for her for the past two months, and he had followed her father every time he went away on business in the hope that he would lead him to her. Today he had reluctantly followed her father to this hotel to discover that as usual he was having a meeting with some businessman, so he was surprised when he saw him come back into the lobby with his daughter. After all the searching, he had finally found her.

Amelia's father Frank was a multi-millionaire, and she was his only daughter. Her mother had died when Amelia was very young and her father became very protective of her. He had employed a nanny to look after her in the daytime, but always made time to make sure he spent the evening with her. Amelia had led a sheltered life in their big mansion and had been home schooled until she was old enough to attend a private senior school, where she had passed A levels in French, German and Spanish. Reluctantly her father agreed to let her attend university, but only because it would enable her to join his business. On starting at university, she felt for the first time that she was really free of her father's over-protectiveness.

Amelia returned to hotel room with many thoughts in her head. Although she was pleased to have seen her father, as she had greatly missed him, she had noticed that he was looking very tired, and was thinking that maybe she should just return home after her summer job had finished. Just then her father rang her to say good night, and she told him that she would be home in eight weeks' time, when her work at the holiday company was finished. Her father was delighted.

As she finished her phone call, there was a knock on the door. As soon as she opened the door the man from the lobby grabbed her and forced her to the floor. Then he covered her mouth with a rag which was soaked in chloroform, and immediately she passed out. The man then put all her belongings in her suitcase. After he had made sure that there was no evidence of a struggle, another man entered the room with a trunk into which they stuffed Amelia's inert body. The first man carried the case down to the lobby and put it into a waiting van, while his accomplice followed with Amelia's suitcase. As he passed the reception desk he handed the clerk a letter addressed to the tour manager explaining that Amelia had been called home as there was a family emergency. Once he had handed over the letter, he joined the other man in the van.

The receptionist on duty had no idea that Amelia had been kidnapped. As far as she was aware, it was just a client checking out of the hotel with his luggage.

The two men drove off at speed into the night. A few miles down the road, the man threw Amelia's mobile phone out of the window.

When Amelia finally woke up she found herself squeezed into some kind of dark, cold box and could tell from the way she was being tossed about that she was in a moving vehicle. She tried her hardest to get out of the box. She was kicking and trying to scream, but because there was masking tape over her mouth and her hands were tied, she could not be heard. All she could do was kick and hope someone would hear her, or that the box she was in would open. She was terrified. She had never felt so alone and frightened in all her life.

Meanwhile a ransom note had been delivered to Frank Driscoll's house saying that they had kidnapped his daughter and he was to pay a million pounds for her safe return. If he wanted her to remain unharmed, he must not inform the police. The date for the handover of the cash was in three days' time, which was enough time for him to get the cash from the vault where he kept it. The kidnappers certainly seemed to know an awful lot of details. With the letter they enclosed a photograph of Amelia, so that her father would know the threat was real and had to be taken seriously.

Frank was horrified when he opened the letter, but he knew exactly what he had to do. He immediately went to his study and opened a secret door hidden behind the bookcase. It led to a small room in which there was a desk with a computer, which he switched on. Immediately a bleep sounded on the computer and a map appeared with a flashing symbol. The symbol was not moving, indicating that the transmitter was stationary. Frank had always been concerned that someone would try to kidnap his daughter, so he had taken precautions. He was a senior agent with the CIA. He had a tracker installed in her phone and another small tracker implanted under her skin. The one under the skin was on the back of her arm under a small birthmark and had been put in by injection when she was five. Amelia knew nothing about it, and had no idea that on his orders the CIA was monitoring her with the tracker. They also had a similar device set up for her father.

As soon as Frank worked out where his daughter was being held, he phoned his friend at the CIA and they immediately arranged for a task force to go there. At midnight the next day the task force surrounded the small cottage in a remote farmyard and stormed the premises. They arrested three men and a woman, who turned out to be Amelia's old nanny. They found Amelia in a small room, tied up on the floor and wearing a blindfold, cold and frightened but safe and well. All four were arrested, and Amelia was taken back to her father.

After Amelia had had a few weeks to recover from her ordeal, her father decided to tell her the truth about his business. It had been a front for CIA activities all along. He had been a field agent when he was younger, but now he was too old for that he ran his own business from his office. Money was sent by the CIA, who used his business as a front for agents to contact when they needed help or were in any danger. The information was then passed onto Amelia's father, who informed the CIA.

A small team ran the IT side of the company's business, totally unaware of her father's secret. The consultants who worked in the outer office were always told that if a Mr or Mrs X phoned and quoted a certain code they were to be put through immediately to her father. The operators were told that they were important shareholders and were to be dealt with immediately and personally by him, and if he was away from the office they should transfer calls immediately to his mobile phone. Usually agents would contact him directly on his mobile, but they also had the office number if they were concerned that their calls were being monitored or if they could be overheard. He would then arrange the help they needed.

The men who had kidnapped Amelia had no idea that the CIA were using the premises. They assumed that the nanny who had given them the information about her had talked to someone and had informed the police. Fortunately the nanny was not aware of the tracker. They were just a gang of criminals who thought it would be easy to steal from some rich old banker. Little did they know what they were up against. They were all charged with kidnapping and were sentenced to 10 years' imprisonment.

After a year of intensive training, Amelia also became a CIA operator, and she loved it. After ten years travelling the world as an active agent, she was finally able to work alongside her father, being taught everything he knew. Finally, when he retired, she took over her father's role and contacts in the business. She was a very skilled agent and much enjoyed her new job, which was much more rewarding than working as a holiday rep, and also involved using her languages.

When her father finally retired, Amelia never had to worry where he was. After all, she could always check his tracker.

SECOND CHANCES

—❦—

As she stood on the bridge watching two swans swimming past with their little family following on behind, Monica Thomas thought how gracious they looked gliding gently along without a care in the world. She knew that although they looked very calm and stately on the surface, underneath they were paddling like mad to keep moving.

She could identify with those swans. To anyone watching, she was just an old woman taking photos, but in truth she was like the swans; she looked calm, but underneath her mind was paddling like mad, alert to anything that could happen. Although she was taking photographs of the swans, they were not her real subject. That was the man strolling along the riverbank with a young blonde.

Monica was a single woman, and she had previously worked for an escort agency. She had no family, but she had managed to save most of her earnings, which enabled her to buy an office which had a large flat above it where she lived. Her company was a small agency which employed 'honey-trappers', women who are paid by other women to check to see if their husbands or partners were unfaithful. Although she enjoyed working as a honey-trapper, it was a young woman's game, and not many men would turn their heads to look at her now that she had reached her fifties. So she had decided to start her own business and pass on her expertise to new and younger girls.

The girls never had sex with the men they were trapping; they would just flirt to see if the men were prepared to be unfaithful if given the chance, taking photos as evidence. She had six young girls working for her now. These days she mainly worked in the office, as she was now past her prime for this sort of career.

That had all changed when she had received a phone call from a woman who had explained that she was afraid her husband was having an affair. He had changed and become very distant with her recently. She wanted Monica's agency to make an appointment for a honey-trapper to investigate. As it was summertime, some of Monica's girls were away on holiday; in fact as a rule they did not usually work during July. This case was different, so Monica decided to visit the lady in her home herself.

The next day Monica visited her client, Mrs Janice Western, at her home, and drove through the gated house to arrive at a beautiful four-bedroomed detached house. On entering the hallway she was greeted by Mrs Western, who ushered her into the lounge area. After Monica had finished taking all the details, she felt that she really had to help this lovely lady. Although she knew Mrs Western was 65 years old, she looked no older than Monica. She was beautifully dressed, and her makeup and hair were perfect. It transpired that since her husband had retired he had become very withdrawn and went out golfing every day, leaving Mrs Western alone.

Janice, as Mrs Western insisted Monica should call her, had retired six months before her husband, and she enjoyed an active social life. When her husband had retired she had stopped seeing some of her friends as she had wanted to spend more time with him, but it appeared that he did not want to spend time with her. They had always led very separate lives, as they were both career people and often went out to separate parties and had different friends. They had both been very happy with this arrangement, but now that he had also retired and Janice wanted them to do more together, he never seemed to be available.

One day when Janice was in town shopping she bumped into an old friend who worked in the jewellery shop. This woman had commented that she hoped Janice liked the beautiful diamond bracelet that her husband had bought her for her birthday last week. Needless to say Janice was astounded, as she had not received any such gift. She did not want her friend to know this, so she simply said, "Yes, it was beautiful, and so unexpected!"

After a while her friend said her goodbyes and left Janice wondering what the story was behind the bracelet. On her birthday her husband, George, gave her two tickets for a cruise, as he knew she had always wanted to go on one. Janice was delighted, and asked when they were going, but to her horror he said that he was not going with her. He explained that he had thought she would prefer to go with her best friend, Margery. He had already contacted Margery and arranged the trip with her, saying it was a surprise. As a special treat he was happy to pay for both of them to have this trip together.

The cruise was for two weeks, starting on the 1st July; hence her hasty telephone call to Monica on the 28th June for someone to watch her husband while she was away. Monica arranged to visit her that day to get as much information as she could, including a recent photo of George.

Today was the 3rd of July, and every day since her meeting with Janice Monica had waited patiently outside Janice's house on the opposite side of the road in order to follow George, to no avail. However, today she was in luck. She managed to follow him in his car to a bridge over a river. As she followed him on foot from a discreet distance, she saw him cross the bridge and meet up with a young blonde girl. He was carrying a small picnic basket and a red rug. They stopped, walked across the grass to a quiet spot and sat down on the blanket, where he opened a bottle of champagne and poured it into two glasses. He then opened a box of expensive chocolates, which they shared as they sat on the river bank talking.

A little later, she saw him reach into the basket again. He opened a box and produced a glittering bracelet, which he placed on the woman's wrist.

Monica zoomed the camera lens in and managed to get some good photographs.

After an hour they started to pack up to leave. Immediately Monica slipped away, heading back to the car park to wait for them to appear and get into George's car. She followed at a safe distance as they drove into a very smart hotel. Monica managed to park in a quiet corner where she would not be noticed. She always kept a change of clothes in her car so that she could easily change her disguise in case she was ever spotted. She climbed into the back of her car and changed into a smart pair of navy trousers and a navy and white striped top. Then she piled her hair up into a French plait and put on some lipstick. In a few moments she had transformed herself from an old lady to a younger, more chic figure, better suited to fitting in with the hotel's elegant surroundings.

The hotel lobby was the most opulent she had ever seen. It had huge palm trees and waterfalls with lots of large plants, ideal for a discreet encounter. She managed to find a small table and chair in the lobby and started to look at the menu whilst at the same time watching the couple. After they had finished signing in at the reception desk they came and sat near to Monica. They ordered champagne and strawberries. After a while they left to go up to their room.

The waiter came up to ask Monica if she would like something from the menu and she replied "Yes, I would like a large cappuccino and a slice of carrot cake please". She was not sure how long she would have to wait to see if or when the couple left. After she had ordered, she asked the waiter if he knew the name of the gentleman who was sitting at the other table, saying she thought he looked familiar and that he might be a friend of her brothers. She explained to the waiter that she did not want to introduce herself in case she had the wrong person. The waiter replied "Oh that's Mr Western. He and his daughter are regulars here". Monica then replied, "Oh sorry, my brother's friend is Mr Smith, but he looks very much like him". The waiter smiled and proceeded to fetch her coffee and cake.

Monica was astounded. His daughter? Janice had told her that the Westerns didn't have any children. The girl might be *his* daughter, but she certainly wasn't Janice's. She felt very sad that Janice, who was such a lovely lady, had a husband who had been keeping a daughter secret from her.

Monica stayed for a while and enjoyed her coffee and cake in the relaxing atmosphere of the lobby.

Then she decided to leave. As she was walking out on her way to the ladies' toilets, the desk clerk answered the telephone. When she heard him say, "Good evening Mr Western, how I can help you?" she stopped, picked up a magazine from a pile on a table in the lobby and pretended to read it while she tried to listen to the conversation.

"Yes, Mr Western, I can order a taxi for both of you," the clerk went on. Then after a pause: "Yes, that is now all booked for tomorrow morning at 9 am, going to Heathrow Airport, Terminal Five."

Monica really wanted to find out where Mr Western and his secret daughter were going, but she needed to leave the hotel now, as it was obvious that the pair were staying the night. She drove home wondering what to do. She could of course just turn up at the airport and see what flight they were catching, or she could try to get on the same flight so that she could follow them. However that would be difficult to organize at such short notice, and if the flight was already fully booked she wouldn't be able to go anyway. Plus she would have to charge Janice for all the expense.

When she arrived home she decided to report back to Janice and let her decide what she should do next. She sent an email telling her that her husband was travelling abroad the next day, and asked her what she wished her to do. Monica then had a relaxing hot bubble bath and opened a bottle of wine and settled down to watch a film on Netflix.

An hour later she had a reply email from Janice asking her to follow him wherever he went, regardless of the cost. Immediately, Monica had to do some research. She knew that only British Airways flew from Terminal 5, but how on earth would she find out where they were going? It could be anywhere.

She decided to phone British Airways at the terminal and use some excuse to see if she could find out what flight they had checked into. She put on an elderly, shaky voice and managed to speak to a very helpful official, explaining that she was hoping to go to the airport to see her son off, but she had forgotten what flight he was going on. She gave the gentleman his name and said "I really want to surprise him and turn up at the airport to see him off, but I am afraid I just can't remember where he said he was going". After a little while the official came back with the answer. He said, "Yes, your son has booked a first-class ticket going to Paris at 11 am". After thanking him for his help, Monica hung up.

She then started to see if she could buy a ticket to Paris. There were still two seats available in Economy on the same flight, so she quickly booked one of them. She then ordered a taxi to collect her to take her to the airport for 8 am. She quickly packed a small overnight bag, found her passport and printed off her boarding pass. Then she set her alarm for 7 am and went to bed.

The following morning at the airport, she spotted Mr Western and his daughter in the queue at the airline's check-in area. She knew she would not see them in the waiting area, because they were in the first-class lounge and Monica was in the economy section. The next time she saw them was in baggage reclaim. She got as near as she could to them, and found that Mr Western was on the phone booking a taxi to take them to the Hilton Hotel. What a breakthrough! Now all Monica had to do was hope she could get a room at the Hilton.

She then hailed a taxi and asked to be taken to the Hilton hotel. She arrived just in time to see the couple entering the lift to go to their rooms. She now had to try to get a room herself. After what seemed to take ages, she managed to book a single room for two nights, which she felt would be enough time. Fortunately she was given a room with a balcony overlooking the front of the hotel, so she could see who was coming and going. She enquired about the restaurant and booked herself a single table for her evening meal for 8 pm. She then had a shower and changed before going down to sit in the lobby so she could watch them unobserved.

What surprised her then was that they met up with three other people in the lobby. After greeting each other the group started to leave the hotel. Monica followed them through the swing doors, where they hailed a taxi to the Eiffel Tower. Monica then hailed another taxi and followed them to the Eiffel Tower.

At the Tower, she was able to take plenty of photos of Mr Western, the girl and the rest of the group. This was easy, as they imagined she was just another tourist taking photographs of the scenery. After they had finished sightseeing the group of five all returned to the hotel restaurant, where they ate together.

Monica sat at her table and then spoke to the waiter. "They look a happy group," she commented. He replied, "Yes, that's a small family dinner. They've got a wedding tomorrow."

Monica was shocked. A wedding party? What was happening? Was Mr Western's daughter getting married? On further investigation she discovered that it was to be a small wedding in a private area which had been cordoned off for the event.

That evening, the staff were busy setting up candles, chairs and decorations for the celebrations. Monica had a quiet word with one of the waitresses, who said that the wedding was to take place at 11 am tomorrow after an early breakfast at 8 am for the guests. She asked if she would be allowed to see the venue, saying that she was thinking of using it for her own daughter's wedding. The waitress was reluctant, but finally she agreed to give her a tour after she had finished with the decorations, as long as there were not many staff around.

Monica was amazed when she saw the arrangements for the wedding. The white satin chairs, the chandeliers and the gardens were beautiful. There were white and pink flowers in high vases everywhere, which was just breathtaking. It was an exquisite setting and must be costing a fortune. Monica knew that she would not be able to get away with taking photos of the ceremony, because she would be noticed, as it was a very small wedding with only 12 guests, but she did take a few photographs of the venue for Janice.

The next morning she made sure she was sitting where she could see the guests arriving. What a grand occasion it was. All the guests looked so beautiful. Eventually the bride arrived, walking down the winding stairway with a gentleman, and yes, it was Mr Western, who looked every bit the proud father with his daughter on his arm. The bride looked stunning, and the diamond bracelet sparkled on her wrist as it caught the light. Monica managed to get a quick photo of them coming down the stairs and then hastily walked away, so it was not too obvious that she had done it.

She then went to the reception desk to book her taxi to return home the next morning. She felt so sad that Janice's husband had kept this from her. Monica was not looking forward to telling Janice that her husband was not only guilty of having an affair, but that he had a daughter and he had set up the cruise for her so that he could give her away on her wedding day.

As Monica was settling her bill, she asked if the wedding party was staying at the hotel and the receptionist told her they were staying for two more days. Monica thanked him and went to her room. The next day she returned home, exhausted.

The following morning Monica typed up her report and finished downloading the photos. She then placed all the information in a large envelope and put it into her safe. Monica always asked her clients to come to her office to see evidence rather than posting it or giving it to the client, so that there would be no possibility of the husband or partner accidentally seeing them.

That question was still playing on Monica's mind: why was George Western hiding his daughter from his wife? She felt that perhaps she should do some more research and see if she could find any further evidence. But where should she start? That was the problem. As Mr Western met his daughter in a public place and not at her home, this made Monica wonder if she should at least try and find out more about this mystery daughter. She had photos of the woman. Maybe she could try and locate her through Facebook, although she really needed a name for that. She decided to look to see if Mr Western was on Facebook and if there was a link to her there. She found his profile easily enough, but there was no link. However, she did discover that he was a member of a local golf club. She decided to look up the club's website to see if she could see any pictures that might help.

Eventually, after going through pages and pages of photographs of golf tournaments, she saw a group picture in which Mr Western was standing next to his daughter. Eureka!

She had found the girl. Now all she had to do was

try and find her name. A little more work and she had it; Miss Olivia Johnson, one of the club organiser for the tournaments. This was the reason then that Mr Western went to play golf every day – he was seeing his daughter. Monica wondered how long it had been going on like this, or if they had they just recently got back into contact. Had he discovered her working at the golf club by chance and found she was his daughter, or had he always known about her? These were the questions going around and around in Monica's mind.

The next step was to see if Olivia was on Facebook. Eventually Monica found her. The most recent update stated that her 'father' had passed away eight months ago. Trawling back through her photos and reading her posts, Monica found lots of photos of her and her family. Her mother was called Maria, and she was married to the father, whose name was Martin Johnson. Olivia was their second and younger child. She had an older brother called Jonathan, who was married.

She started reading through old posts, and found lots of photos of Olivia and Mr Western at various birthday functions over the years. It would appear he had known about his daughter for many years. One photo described Mr Western as her godfather. The latest post was a photo of her on her wedding day with him, saying her godfather had played an important part in her life and had been a great influence on her, and that she was grateful that he was able to give her away as her father had previously passed away. She said she was now looking forward to spending her honeymoon in Monte Carlo, after seeing her guest off after a truly beautiful wedding in Paris.

Monica downloaded the photos and comments and added them to the collection of papers in the envelope for Janice. Now her head was buzzing with questions. Was Mr Western her godfather, or her father? Was he still having an affair with his daughter's mother? Was Olivia's father aware that Olivia was not his daughter? Why had Mrs Western not been invited to the wedding?

The more Monica thought about it, the more convinced she was that Olivia was indeed Mr Western's daughter. But how was Janice going to take the news that her husband had been keeping such a secret for her all these years?

The morning had arrived that Monica was dreading. Janice had rung the day before to say that she was back from her cruise and that she would like to make an appointment the next day to see her on Friday. They arranged to meet at two o'clock. Monica had the envelope ready and had placed a tray of tea and biscuits ready on the coffee table by the couch, together with a small box of tissues ready to hand, just in case.

Monica invited Janice to sit down and began to explain what she had discovered. She then handed her the envelope. Janice's hands were shaking as she went through all the information and looked at the photographs. Monica poured her another cup of tea with extra sugar, and Janice sipped it gratefully and continued looking through the evidence. When she saw the photograph of the bride's mother she gasped, and the tears began to flow.

"That's Maria," she said. "She was George's secretary. I've known her for years. We used to meet up sometimes on the odd occasions when I went to one of his works parties." She went on to say that Maria had worked with her husband for years, but had left the company a long time ago, and as far as she was concerned they had lost contact with her.

At this point Janice completely broke down. It now seemed that her husband had been having an affair with Maria, perhaps for some years. Monica was so distressed to see this lovely lady in so much pain that she decided to just sit quietly and let Janice take it all in. While she waited for Janice to compose herself, she left to make a fresh pot of tea and opened up a packet of cupcakes. She was very concerned that Janice would collapse with shock, as she was very pale, but gradually she began to regain her composure.

When she was more settled, Monica asked her if she would like her to call a taxi to take her home. Janice agreed and said that her husband was away on a golfing tournament for the weekend, so she would have time to think more clearly at home on her own. Monica told her to contact her any time over the weekend if she needed someone to talk to or do anything to help her.

All weekend Monica was thinking about Janice. On Monday she was relieved to have a phone call from her asking if she would accompany her to her solicitors, as she wanted to change her will. On arrival at the solicitor's office, Monica advised her not to change her will immediately but just to ask the solicitor for copies of both her will and her husband's, so they could see if her husband had made any changes behind her back. After explaining to the solicitor that she had misplaced her own copy, she also asked for a copy of her husband's will, as they had made them at the same time. The solicitor was happy to oblige. He made photocopies of both wills and handed them over to her.

The two women then got a taxi back to Monica's flat to look at the wills in detail. It transpired that Janice was the one who had most of the money. She was from a rich family, and as an only child she had inherited all her parents' wealth. She had married George soon after their deaths. The original will provided for everything Janice owned to be left to her husband, and it amounted to a large sum of money. Her husband on the other hand had willed half his money to her and the rest to his 'goddaughter', Olivia Georgina Johnson. The house they lived in was in Janice's name only because she had bought it outright with the money from her parent's estate when they were married, and she had never got around to adding her husband's name to the deeds.

As soon as she saw he had left half to Olivia, Janice knew that she must be his daughter and not his goddaughter; an additional clue was Olivia's middle name, Georgina.

Monica asked Janice what she was planning to do now.

"Well," said Janice, "the first thing I need to do is to start divorce proceedings. To be honest, if he had told me about Olivia I would not have minded as much as I minded about his affair. The worst part is that he has kept it a secret from me all these years. I need to think about my priorities. And the first thing I'm going to do is to contact Maria."

She explained that before she started divorce proceedings, she needed to know if the affair was still going on and whether Olivia was indeed his daughter. The only way she could find that out was to ask Maria. She felt that if he asked her husband he would just give her the run around, as he had been so clever at hiding things from her for so long. She felt she had a better chance with Maria.

Monica said she was happy for her to meet Maria and for her to use her office if she preferred somewhere neutral to meet where they could talk privately.

"I think I'd like you to check on Maria first," replied Janice. "I'd like to know where she lives now, and if George visits her regularly. Before I meet her I'd like to have some facts."

Monica agreed to undertake this mission, but first she wanted Janice to wait at least two weeks before challenging her husband or starting any divorce proceedings, so that she could collect as much information as she could.

So now Monica had to find out where Maria was living. At least she had her surname, Johnson, so she could now look up her address and start building a report on her findings.

She found that Maria had a lovely country home called Willow Cottage with sweeping fields all around. It was in a very small village, so Monica had to be careful not to be noticed. She decided to present herself as an older woman, so she put on a grey wig and carried a walking stick.

On arrival she found a local tea shop and ordered a pot of tea. She told the waitress that she was looking to rent a cottage nearby for a few weeks as she was recovering from an operation and wanted somewhere to stay where it was quiet and where she could recover. The waitress said that she knew a couple of people were looking for lodgers and that they had put up advertisements in the post office window. With this in mind, Monica set off to look. To her great good fortune, she found an advertisement inviting lady lodgers to apply for a room in a house which happened to be directly opposite Willow Cottage.

The door of the house was opened by an elderly lady who introduced herself as Mrs Pearson and said that she had lived in the village for many years. She had just lost her husband and was hoping to have a lodger in to help her financially, and also to have someone else in the house for some company. She had two bedrooms available and invited Monica to choose which one she would like. Monica explained that she would like to stay for just a short time initially, to see if she settled in. Although she preferred the back bedroom with the views over the countryside, she opted for the front bedroom, which overlooked the road. It was essential for her to be able to see anyone who was visiting Maria, and the room would give her a good view, as she could clearly see the driveway and the front door.

After telling Mrs Pearson that she would like to move in for two weeks initially, she went home to pack her things for a short stay. On her return she explained that she needed to have plenty of rest in her room, as she was recovering from an illness. This would also explain why she needed to be in her bedroom most of the time in the future. The real reason, of course, was that she wanted to be able to watch Maria's house.

Monica told Mrs Pearson that her name was Maureen, and paid her in cash for the rent for two weeks. After she had unpacked her small case, she opened her laptop and emailed Janice, explaining her intentions and telling her that she would keep her informed.

One thing Monica knew about old ladies was that they love to talk, so she went downstairs to the kitchen, where Mrs Pearson was preparing a cup of tea with some homemade scones. She ushered Monica into the front room and started to talk all about her life in the village. Monica nodded and agreed with everything. Eventually she asked her if her neighbours had been living there a long time too.

She didn't have to ask twice. After that, she could hardly shut Mrs Pearson up. She knew the Johnson family very well and told Monica about Mr Johnson's death, with all the details, right down to who had attended the funeral. She said that their son Jonathan was living in Scotland with his wife, so he didn't visit much, and that her daughter Olivia had been at university studying, but after getting her degree, she had fallen in love and had recently got married in Paris. Olivia was now living with her husband about 20 miles away, and she had a very good job working at the local golf club and often visited her mother. She said that they were a lovely family and the children were both very lucky to have such loving parents. Nothing Mrs Pearson said, however, gave any hint that Olivia was not Martin Johnson's biological daughter.

It seemed that Maria lived at home practically all the time. She went out only to visit the local shops or to play tennis at the local club. With Janice's approval, Monica decided to arrange to meet up with her and see what she could find out.

Apparently, every Thursday there was a cake sale in the local church hall and everyone attended. Mrs Pearson had made a large coffee and walnut cake and insisted on Monica coming to the fete. Within minutes she spotted Maria and made her way over to her stall of cupcakes after some general chit chat, mainly regarding recipes. Maria seemed to be a very nice lady and didn't seem to Monica to be the type to sleep around and have affairs. However, she needed to keep her options open and keep her thoughts to herself.

The next day Monica sent an email to Janice informing her of the latest situation, though there was not a great deal to say. The same day Maria invited Monica and Mrs Pearson over for tea. Her cottage was cosy and comfortable and was decorated with beautiful things. There were pictures on the mantelpiece of her husband and her children at various ages, including wedding photographs. Maria talked about her husband and said how sad she was that he had missed his daughter's wedding. It seemed to Monica that she was still very much in love with her husband. It didn't appear that she was lying or hiding any secrets. Although Monica still continued to watch the cottage, the only visitors Maria seemed to have were local friends. Monica followed her to the tennis club too, but she did not meet up with any male friends.

Soon Monica's time in the village was coming to an end, and she needed to go back home. On her return, she phoned Janice and arranged a meeting for the next Monday. She spent the day writing up her report and downloading the few photos of Maria she had managed to get.

After seeing the material Monica had gathered, Janice felt that she should now go and visit Maria. She did so the following week. Maria welcomed Janice and was thrilled to see her again after such a long time. Janice felt it best to be honest, so after the pleasantries were exchanged, she asked Maria about her daughter. Then she said that she had found out that her own husband was Olivia's godfather, and she wanted to know why.

At this point Maria burst into tears. "So you know!" she said. "Oh Janice, I've been dreading this day! We wanted to tell you, honestly, but George thought it would be too cruel."

It transpired that many years before, she and George had had a one-night stand after getting drunk at a works party. Both had deeply regretted it the next day and agreed to never speak of it again, but then Maria found out that she was pregnant. They were both in shock, knowing that the news would wreck both their marriages, and Maria already had a son aged three and loved her husband very much. It was just a drunken mistake. George wanted a DNA test done to see if he was the father, and it confirmed that he was. He said the news would devastate his wife, who was already distressed over not being able to provide him with a child, so he suggested that she should let her husband believe it was his and asked Maria if he could be her godfather; that way he could see her growing up and provide for her when necessary, but as her godfather rather than her father. This had worked very well. Her husband had no idea about what had happened, and he adored his daughter. Olivia did not know that George was her father, and they had both vowed that she would never know.

Janice was shocked to hear this, but she was also pleased that it was just a one-off affair and that he had kept his promise to be there for his daughter, which must have been very hard for him because he was protecting Janice from the truth.

Janice asked Maria if her husband had had other affairs, and Maria was outraged at the suggestion. She said, "No, he never saw anyone else before or after. After that night he never looked at another woman and he worked harder than ever so he could provide for his daughter and for you" She said George had always said Janice was his world, and her happiness was the most important thing to him.

Maria said that now Janice knew the truth, she would love her to become part of Olivia's life too, if she could find it in her heart to forgive them both. Janice said this was too much to take in at the moment, but she would think about it.

"Olivia often asks after you," said Maria. "George always said that you chose the presents and sent your love, but you had a very important position at work and that you had to work very long hours, which helped to explained why you couldn't visit on special occasions. All the cards sent to Olivia were always signed from both of you." She explained that George only ever visited on Olivia's birthdays to take her gifts. Maria had little contact with him.

Maria explained that when her husband had died,

things had changed and Olivia had turned to George and relied even more on him as her godfather. With the coming wedding George was delighted when Olivia asked him to stand in for her as her father. "Olivia wanted you to come too, Janice," she said. "But George explained that you were unable to, because you would be away on a cruise with your best friend."

Janice was exhausted after this exchange. She booked herself in at the local hotel, where she had a bath and eventually fell asleep from pure exhaustion.

The next day, after a week of thinking of nothing else, Janice made a decision. Her husband had made one mistake, and he had kept it a secret to protect her. He had provided for his daughter, which explained why he was insistent on working long hours, including weekends. He was making sure that he could provide for both his daughter and his wife. During the last six months, when she had felt he was being distant and not wanting to be with her, it was because he was helping his daughter, who was grieving for her father, not because he was avoiding spending time with his wife. Janice felt that he must have been under enormous strain in having to keep this secret from her all these years.

One evening after he had finished dinner, Janice

asked him to come and sit with her, saying she wanted to discuss something with him. George had no idea what was about to happen, but when Janice finished speaking he broke down. Janice had never seen him cry before. He was always in control of his feelings, as he was a strong character, but at that moment he was a broken man. Between the sobs he just kept saying, "I am so sorry, please forgive me! I cannot live without you, you are my world".

Eventually, after he had calmed down, he started to relate his story in full. Finally he told Janice, "I have never since slept with any other woman. I learnt my lesson after that night and I never wanted to cheat or hurt you again. I am truly sorry. I hope you can forgive me. Please give me a second chance to put things right. I would really love for you to meet my daughter one day, if you can find it in your heart to forgive me".

Two months later George met up with Olivia and told her that his wife had now retired, so they were going to go on a world cruise together. When they returned, he would like Olivia to come over with her husband and meet her. Olivia said she would love to and they arranged a date. Maria, George and Janice all agreed to keep to the same story, so that Olivia was not hurt by the truth.

After they had met for the first time, Janice was overwhelmed by the gratitude Olivia showed towards her, thanking her for sending her such lovely gifts and cards over the years. She said she was only sorry that she had not met her earlier. Janice apologised for not making more time to see her, but said that now she was retired she was going to make sure they met up regularly, so promised to meet up every three months. Janice became very fond of Olivia, and loved her as if she had been her own daughter.

During their next visit to see George and Janice, Olivia announced that she was going to have a baby. Everyone was ecstatic with this announcement, especially when she asked Janice if she would be the baby's godmother. Janice wept tears of joy. She might not have become a mother, but she was going to make sure she was the best godmother this child could ever have. As soon as the child was born, she would also make sure that her goddaughter or godson would be provided for in her will, along with Monica, for without her she would not have been a part of this lovely family. For now, she was going to enjoy spending time with her husband, who was taking her out on lots of trips and thoroughly spoiling her. They were now both enjoying their retirement and excited about the future with their new family.

They decided to visit Scotland and meet up with Jonathan and his wife. Janice sent an email to Monica updating her and explaining what had happened and saying that without her help she would never have had the family she had so desired. She said she believed that everyone should be given a second chance in life, because her second chance had been the best decision she had ever made. She thanked Monica for the support she had given to her at the most vulnerable time in her life, when she had so desperately needed expert advice and friendship.

She asked Monica if they could remain friends and meet up sometimes socially, as she felt that she was not just an employee but a friend of the family now. She also said that on Christmas Eve the whole family were coming to stay at her house and they were having a party, and she asked Monica if she would like to come too.

When Monica read the email she was delighted that the adventure had had such a good outcome and that Janice was able to forgive her husband and start a new life. She was also pleased that Janice wanted to remain friends, as she felt they had really bonded and became close over the past few weeks. As Monica had no family, she felt moved that Janice was willing to have her as a part of her life. She was also looking forward to finally meeting the people who she had so far seen only through a camera lens. Maybe she too had been given a second chance of happiness by becoming a small part of a family she never had.

She went to her safe and got out all the evidence of the Western Case and shredded it. Realising that there was still life at 50, she cleared out her wardrobe of all her old clothes and went shopping for some new ones. She then made an appointment at the hairdressers to have her hair restyled and her nails done. Soon it would be time to meet up with Janice to go Christmas shopping, and to buy a special dress for that party.

SECRETS

The clock in the hallway of the little thatched cottage chimed three o'clock just as Amanda's phone rang. She took the call, listened intently, said "thank you" and pressed the end call button. Then she flopped exhausted into the nearside chair.

It was at that moment that reality and relief kicked in. She knew it was finally over, and the tears began to flow. She had not cried for over a year, but now the tears were falling in an avalanche and she was sobbing from deep inside her soul. Was she finally free from this nightmare?

Amanda Hawkins had been married to Tom

Pritchard for three years. They had first met in London at a bar she had not been to before. She was out with her friends, and during the evening she was introduced to a young man who was introduced to her as Tom Pritchard. They started chatting, and then at the end of the evening they swapped phone numbers. After many texts and phone calls, they started to date. Everything went so well. All her friends loved Tom. He was very charming, and everyone thought he was a great catch. So did Amanda herself.

She did not know that Tom had a dark secret that nobody knew about, one which he hid very well.

They were married on the beach in Greece with just a few close friends, mainly from Amanda's side. Tom had explained that his parents had died in a car accident a few years before. Amanda had been adopted at an early age, but her adoptive parents had also died, so she had great empathy with Tom and this brought them much closer.

Tom was an only child, and so was Amanda. He had inherited his parents' large house in rural Wales, but he worked in London as an architect, so he rarely visited the family home. After the wedding he told her that he wanted them to live in his family home in Wales. He said he had secured a new job in Cardiff, which was only half an hour's drive from the house.

Amanda was not happy that he had not told her about the job before he had accepted it. She was not very keen to move either, as she wanted to continue her work in interior design in London and to be near her friends, but when Tom got upset that she did not want to move to Wales, she gave in and agreed to go. After all she loved him, and maybe she could find a job in interior designing in Wales, or even work as a secretary, since she had both sets of skills.

The first year was wonderful. Tom gave Amanda a free hand to change the house as she wished, and it was an interior designer's dream. She loved being able to choose all the furnishings and make it into a beautiful home. Tom's only stipulation was that she was not to go up to the attic, because he said it was filthy and there wasn't much there but dust. Also it was a very steep climb up on the ladder and he didn't want her to fall. This did not concern Amanda, as the house had six large bedrooms, three with en-suites, and two acres of land where sheep grazed. It also had a beautiful large fountain and fine rose gardens, so the views from the bedrooms were just breathtaking.

For their first anniversary Tom booked a beautiful villa in Greece near to the beach where they had got married. They spent two weeks in this beautiful place, but during the second week Amanda was starting to get bored, as it was just like being at home. There were no other people for miles around, just them in a huge villa. It had its own pool, so there was no need to go anywhere else. She felt isolated again, even though Tom was with her. They did use the local restaurant and markets, but it was very limited as to what you could do or buy.

Then Amanda brought up the suggestion that she might return to work and maybe looking for a job in Wales. This was not received well by Tom. He announced that he felt they should be starting a family, and there was no time like the present. Without further ado he whisked her off up to the bedroom, carrying a bottle of champagne. Amanda was shocked, as she was not ready for children, but Tom as usual was so excited that she did not want to spoil this romantic moment.

On their return home, Tom started becoming obsessed with pregnancy tests and bought them every month, and every month the results were the same: negative. He suggested that Amanda should go for tests, because he was sure that her failure to conceive could not be anything to do with him. Amanda underwent extensive tests, which established that everything was normal. Eventually after much persuading, Tom agreed to take a sperm sample for testing and this came back as fertile, so there was no problem with either of them. They just had to be patient and keep trying.

But after over a year of trying, Amanda still was not pregnant. Tom was becoming increasingly agitated and suggested that she was not taking enough care of herself and that was why she was not getting pregnant. He was now like a different man. His lovemaking became more demanding and more violent, almost to the point of rape. It was as if he was punishing her for not getting pregnant. This made Amanda start to doubt her ability to conceive children and she felt even more trapped in the house, so she decided that for her own sanity she needed to get a job. The local paper was lying on the kitchen table, so while she had her coffee she skipped through to the jobs page to see if there was anything going. She could see nothing suitable, until she turned the next page and saw that a local solicitor called Parry was advertising for a part-time secretary just two days a week, 9-5. This, thought Amanda, would be perfect.

She immediately phoned the number in the advertisement and arranged an interview with Mr Parry to take place in a few days' time. She was not going to tell her husband yet; she preferred to wait until she got the job before letting him know, so that they could celebrate together.

At the interview, Amanda was immediately offered the position, and agreed to work on Wednesdays and Fridays. She could not wait to tell Tom her news. But when he came home that evening he was in such a bad mood that she decided not to say anything, but to wait for a better time.

She started the job the following week, and still she had not told him about it. Soon two months had gone by. Tom was very distant with her, apart from when he wanted sex, and now he started going away nearly every other weekend. Amanda did not like the change in him and decided to ask for some advice from the solicitor she was working for, who was a gentle man with years of experience. She felt she could talk to Mr Parry confidentially about anything. He was very kind and he was always giving Amanda praise for her hard work, saying he appreciated all she did.

While she was talking to him, she happened to mention her husband's surname. As soon as she mentioned it, Mr Parry became very anxious. He said to her, "Amanda, you are not safe with that man. You need to consider a divorce".

Amanda was shocked. On the odd occasion when Amanda had mentioned her husband before, she had always referred to him as Tom and said they had met in London, so Mr Parry had assumed he was from there. Locally he was always called Thomas and never Tom. Also, because Amanda had not worked for two years since leaving London, she still had her maiden name on her CV. She had explained at the interview that she had not yet changed her surname, but the solicitor never asked what her new name was, and still knew her only as Amanda Hawkins. She still had a bank account in her maiden name, so her wages were paid into that account.

The solicitor said he knew Thomas's parents well and asked if she knew what had happened to them. She said she had been told that they had been killed in a car accident.

"Yes, but did you know that Thomas was probably responsible for the accident?" asked Mr Parry. "You see, my son-in-law is a police officer, and he's convinced that he had done something to the brakes."

He explained that as a teenager, Tom had had a job as a car mechanic. The solicitor played golf with Thomas's father occasionally and his wife was friends with Thomas's mother. She had confided in him that they were terrified of Thomas's outbursts but just assumed it was a teenage problem and he would eventually get over his mood swings.

"I just wish I had pressed them for more details," Mr Parry went on. "Perhaps if I had done that I might have been able to prevent their deaths."

What was she to do? She decided to make an appointment with Owen, Mr Parry's son-in-law policeman, who was willing to tell her all about the accident. He explained that Thomas' parents car had gone off the road and they had both been killed instantly. On investigation the police had found that the brake pipes appeared to have been cut, although no one could think of any reason why anyone would do this to such an innocent couple. Tom Pritchard was the only one with a motive, and he also had the mechanical knowledge. Of course, he was a slippery character and always had an answer for everything. However, there might be some evidence left lying around in the house. If she could find anything, they would be able to start a new inquiry.

After Amanda had heard this story, she decided to think seriously about starting divorce proceedings.

For the next three months Amanda searched everywhere for anything that might be connected to the accident, without success. Then she remembered the attic. When her husband was planning his next trip to the USA, she told Owen, and together they went up into the attic, where they found two large trunks, both heavily padlocked. Owen managed to break the lock, and inside they found Tom's diaries for the last few years.

They made grim reading. He described how he had murdered his parents and how stupid they were to think they could ever get away from him. In the trunk there was also some children's clothing, a pair of trousers and some toys. The diaries related how Tom had gone with his mother and younger brother to the park. While his mother had her back towards him he had seen his younger brother at the top of the slide and had pulled on his trouser leg, which had caused the child to fall from top to bottom. He wrote that he had laughed out loud at the screams the child made as he fell, but his stupid mother thought he was crying because he was shocked and distressed.

There was more. Tom had also writtten that he had suffocated his new-born baby sister with a pillow and that she was buried under the rose bush by the pond. His parents were devastated at her death, but they believed it had been an accident, as Thomas had said he had not meant to kill her; he had just wanted her to go to sleep as she would not stop crying. She might have only been two days old, but already his parents were doting over her and ignoring him, and he could just not cope with the sense of abandonment. He wanted his parents all to himself.

His parents knew that if they informed the police then Thomas would be in trouble with the law, so they covered the whole affair up and buried the baby in her Moses basket under the rose bush; they had named her Rose. Mr and Mrs Pritchard told their few friends that the baby had been stillborn at home.

Thomas' behaviour seemed to improve as he got older and he went to university to get his degree in architecture. He returned for his 21st birthday and started living back home. One evening, while out in town with his parents, he got drunk and made a flippant remark about having killed his baby sister. His parents were shocked and started to wonder if he needed help. One day Thomas heard them talking in their bedroom and overheard them say that in the morning they were going to see their GP to explain what had happened and to see if he could help Thomas, as they were very concerned that after all these years he was not showing any signs of remorse over killing his sister. His drunken statement made them realise that maybe he needed professional help.

Thomas was furious and started to think how he could stop them. That was what made him decide to cut the brake pipes on their car. The next morning his parents left the house and a few miles from home, going downhill into the valley, the car had gathered speed and run out of control; Mr Pritchard had been unable to stop before hitting a wall. They were both killed instantly. Thomas later recorded in his book that he would rather be alone than with his parents, as they were considering sharing his secret with someone outside the family and possibly sending him away for treatment. He then wrote that he was closing up the house and moving to London.

The next and last entry in the diary explained how Tom had deceived Amanda into thinking he was fertile. He had paid for a fertile sperm sample for the test; in fact he knew perfectly well that he was infertile, but he would have done anything to keep Amanda at home. He knew that if she discovered he could not father children she would suggest adopting a child, so he decided to go with the plan that they were both fertile but just were not able to have children for some other reason. They would go on trying for years. After all she was his and his alone, and he did not want to share her affection with anyone else, even a child.

Upon reading the diaries about the murders, Owen and his colleagues at the police station were convinced that there was now enough evidence for a new trial. Amanda was devastated at this prospect, and the thought of seeing Tom in court filled her with dread. She had to leave home before he returned from his business trip to the USA. She did not want to go anywhere Tom would find her, especially after discovering that he had killed his family and would happily get rid of her if he knew that she had been up in the attic and discovered his secrets. So she left him a note saying that a friend of hers in London was very ill and she was going to look after her for a few weeks; she would text him later.

On his return from the USA, Tom was arrested and charged with murder. Amanda continued to work for Mr Parry, as Tom still had no idea she was working there, and in any case he was kept in custody until the trial. Mr and Mrs Parry kindly invited her to stay with them, so she could live somewhere safe until after the trial. She did not go to court but waited instead for the call from the police officer.

Tom was given a life sentence. But then he wrote to Amanda protesting that he was innocent and asking her to stand by him and to visit him as soon as she could, because he loved her very much and was still anxious to have a child with her! Amanda did not respond to this and filed for a divorce. Tom eventually signed the divorce papers in prison and wrote a letter to her solicitor saying that he had never wanted her anyway, and if he ever got out of prison he would come after her and kill her for divorcing him when he was innocent. The court ruled that the house should be given to Amanda, as she was Tom's legal wife, and because he was serving a life sentence he would not have a share in it.

After selling the house, she helped a new girl to take over her role in the solicitor's office and then finally said goodbye to Mr Parry. She then thanked him and the police for all the help they had given her in bringing Tom to justice and with the selling of the house and organising her new identity and papers.

Finally she loaded up her car with all her possessions and got the car ferry to France, where she had a job interview lined up for an interior designer. She had assumed a new identity, as Miss April Hall.

After she had been working for the company for a while and was established in the job, she settled in to France and bought a charming villa. It was not as grand as the house she had lived in with Tom, but it was hers and she felt safe there. She had no contact with any of her friends in London, and she felt free for the first time in years, and able to live for herself. She would never have to see Tom again.

The Magic of Steam

As the steam train entered the platform, smoke billowed from the funnel and the air smelt strongly of burning coal. It was a fine day in early spring and Emma thought that it was an amazing, magical day. She had never been on a steam train before, and she had loved every minute of this nostalgic trip.

Her granddad had bought her this trip as a gift for her 30th birthday. At first she wasn't sure about it, as she was used to going everywhere by aeroplane; she worked as a flight attendant. Going by train was alien to her, especially if it was an old steam train.

So it was with mixed feelings that she boarded the

train and took her seat. She had brought a couple of books with her to read and a sketch pad, as she loved to draw, and thought that drawing might relieve the boredom she expected with this slow form of travel. However, once she left London she was amazed at the scenery that she saw along the way to Scotland. It was just breathtaking. She started to take photographs of the countryside along the way, thinking she would use them to do some sketches when she got back home. She drank plenty of tea and coffee and enjoyed a good supply of snacks along the way; they were all included with the trip.

When she reached her station in Scotland and stepped down on to the platform, she lingered to take some photos of the magnificent old steam train as it built up steam and chugged out of the station. What a wonderful experience it all was.

As she left the station and walked to the hotel, she felt a lightness in her mood that she had not experienced before. For once, she was relaxed, stress-free and contented. When she checked into her hotel she was surprised at how tired she felt. Unusually for her, she was in bed by 10 pm and within minutes she was sound asleep.

The next day she went for a long walk to explore the mountain scenery around the hotel, and then the following morning it was time to return to London. She went down to eat a hearty cooked breakfast, ready to take the train for her return journey. As she waited on the platform, she noticed a young man standing next to her. He smiled at her and said, "Did you get some good photos of bonnie Scotland then?"

Surprised, she asked, "How do you know I was taking photographs?"

"I was in the next carriage to you on the way up," he replied.

"I'm sorry, I didn't recognise you."

"That's OK, I'm not surprised," he said. "I think you were too busy taking photos and sketching to notice me. I'm Alex McGregor, by the way."

"Emma Nightingale, pleased to meet you."

When the train approached and they climbed aboard, they discovered that this time their seats were in the same carriage. Because she had taken plenty of photographs of the scenery on the way up, she decided to make time on the way home to sit and chat to this charming young man. Her companion proved good company, and the journey seemed to fly by.

Emma had taken the rest of the week off work, so the next day she started on her painting. She wanted to paint a scene from her trip as a thank-you present to her grandfather. She had a small balcony outside her bedroom where she kept her easel, and she did her painting there when the weather was dry. It was a fine day, so she started on a picture of the train.

Several hours had passed before she was happy with it. After leaving it to dry overnight, she mounted it in a frame, then wrapped it in bubble wrap and brown paper with a 'thank you' note inside the parcel to her granddad, and set off for the post office to post it off to him. She knew he loved trains. Now Emma could understand the fascination he felt for them. After her experience she felt she would really like to go on another rail trip; next time, perhaps she would travel through Europe by train instead of always flying over it.

For the rest of the week, Emma continued with her painting. She completed four pictures of the train in different styles and sizes, and three paintings of the Scottish scenery. Finally she framed them all and stacked them by her bed.

That evening she received a text from Alex. They continued to exchange texts for the rest of the evening. It was surprising how quickly the time went and how much they had to talk about. Finally Alex asked if he could see her that weekend. Emma was delighted, and they arranged to meet in London the following day, which was Saturday. She decided to take with her one of her smaller paintings of the train to give to him.

They spent a very pleasant day in London, and when they parted she gave him the painting, with the instruction that he was not to open it until he got home. No sooner had she arrived home than she received a text from Alex, saying he loved the painting and he was going to place it on his bedside table. Emma was thrilled.

She didn't think she would see much more of Alex, as she was due to fly to Australia on the Monday. She found long haul flights were very draining, and it took a while for her to get over them before she was off again on another flight.

However, Alex continued to text her, and she found herself looking forward to the messages more and more. They agreed that as soon as she was back in London for a few days, they would meet up. Alex said that his father was an art dealer and he had very much liked her little painting of the train. He had asked Alex, who worked for him at the gallery, to see if she would be interested in selling any of her paintings. If she had enough to make a collection, he might be willing to display them for her at his studio.

Emma was astounded. She did believe her paintings were good, but she had never imagined that they would be good enough to show in a gallery. This was too good a chance to miss. She agreed to visit Alex's father to discuss it.

A few days later, Emma took a dozen of her recent paintings to Mr McGregor's art gallery, and he looked through them with great interest. He said he would like her permission to show all of them in his shop, and he would put them on sale in return for a small commission. He felt his customers would snap them up. Emma was delighted that a professional actually thought her paintings were good enough for people to buy them, and said she was more than happy to leave them at the gallery.

The next time she saw Alex, he told her that three of her paintings had already been snapped up. Then one a day a few weeks later, he rang to tell her his father had phoned to say that all the paintings had been sold. Emma was thrilled. Mr McGregor had invited her to come to the gallery to collect her cheque, or if she preferred, he could arrange a bank transfer; she opted for the bank transfer. When it came through, it was for more than £1,000. She was delighted.

Alex's job at the gallery was to arrange appointments with clients to look at their art work with a view to selling them in the shop. Little did he know that his chance meeting on the train would provide his father with one of his best suppliers.

Nor had he imagined that he would find romance at the same time. Alex and Emma's relationship blossomed, and a few months later she gave up her job with the airline and went to work full-time for Mr McGregor. She loved working in the shop and was a natural with the clients. She even had more time for her own painting, and she displayed her work in the shop. To Emma this was her ideal job, especially as it was within walking distance of her flat.

Even better, a year later Alex proposed to her during a trip across Europe on the Orient Express, the most romantic experience of her life.

The business was going better and better, and soon Mr McGregor asked Alex and Emma to open another studio in a more rural setting just outside London. Emma loved working in the new town. It was less busy than the London studio, but she worked hard and won many new regular customers. She also continued to paint, and to sell her paintings in the shop.

Emma often looked back to the day when she had taken that steam journey to Scotland. Little had she known that that journey would change her life forever. She would always be grateful to her grandfather for his present to her, for without it she would still be single and working every day as a flight attendant. Steam trains would always have a special place in Emma's heart from now on.

After their wedding two years later, Alex and Emma went on honeymoon by Eurorail, travelling all over Europe. Although they both preferred travelling on the old-fashioned steam trains, they also enjoyed this newer form of travel as they were able to appreciate the countryside of all the many towns and villages as they passed along the way, and the added joy of experiencing it all together.